caillou®

and Rosie's Doll

A Chouette Publishing adaptation
Original text by Francine Allen, based on the animated series
Illustrations: CINAR Animation

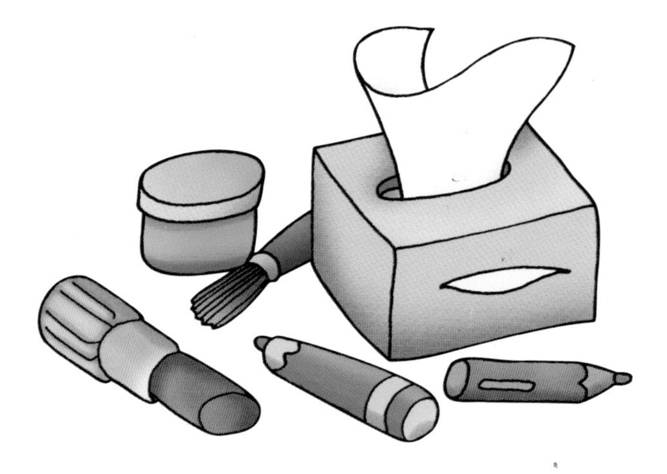

chouette CINAR

"What are you
doing, Mommy?"
asked Caillou.
"Putting on my
makeup," she replied.
"Why?"
"To look nice when
I go out today."

Caillou picked up
a tube of lipstick.
"Oh, Caillou, please
don't play with that."

Ding dong!
"That must be Julie."
Caillou loved it when
Julie came to babysit.

"See you later, you two! Have fun!" Mommy said on her way out.

"Bye, Mommy!"

Caillou and Rosie played for a long time with Julie.
"Caillou, play by yourself, while I get Rosie ready for her nap," said Julie.
"Okay," replied Caillou, picking up Rosie's doll.

Caillou noticed that all the jars and tubes of colorful makeup were still on Mommy's table. He looked at Rosie's doll and had an idea. Caillou went to his room. He chose a few colors from his paint box and sat down on the floor with the doll.

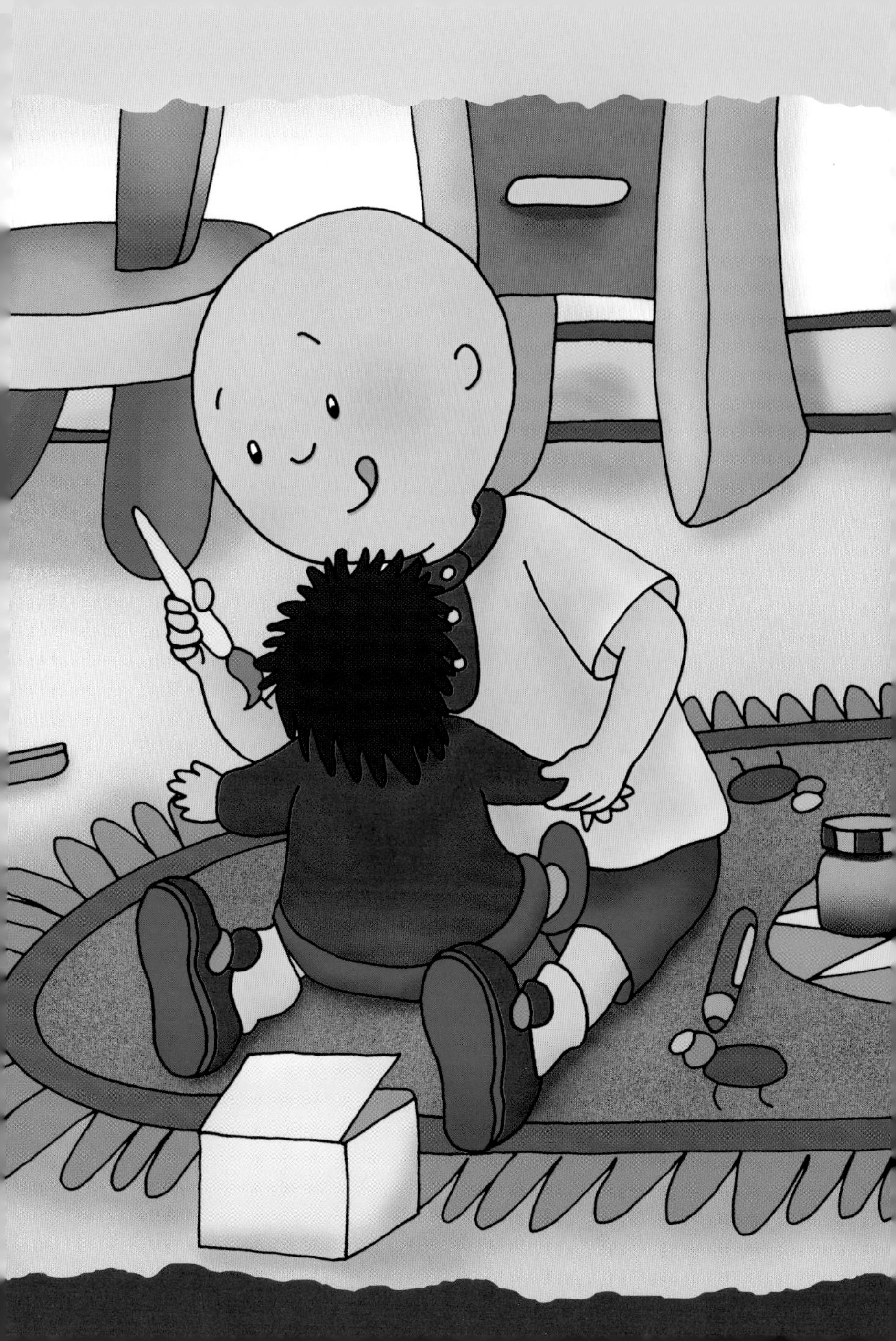

Rosie had finally dozed off. Julie tiptoed out of the room.
"Caillou, where are you?"
When Caillou heard Julie calling, he stopped. He knew he was doing something he shouldn't.

Caillou ran and stuffed the doll in his toy box. He barely had time to sit down on top of it before Julie came into his room.

"Oh, there you are, Caillou," she said. "You were so quiet. What were you doing?"

"Julie! Julie!" Rosie cried out suddenly.
"Oh, Rosie's crying!" said Julie. "Caillou, do you know where Rosie's doll is?"
"No," replied Caillou quietly.
Julie spotted a doll's arm sticking out of the toy box.
"Caillou, is that Rosie's doll I see?"

"Oh dear, Caillou. What did you do?"
"I didn't do it on purpose," Caillou sobbed.

Just then, Mommy came back home.
"Uh-oh, it sounds like someone's done something he shouldn't have."

"Mommy, I didn't do it on purpose! I just wanted to play with Rosie's doll!"

"Come with me Caillou. We'll try to fix it."

Mommy and Caillou
filled the sink with
soapy water.
"Scrub the cheeks
and eyes really well."

"Well, that's a bit better. Let's dry the doll and see what Rosie thinks of her now."

Rosie was very happy to have her doll back.

Caillou was relieved. He hugged Mommy. "I think my little Caillou feels a lot better too!" she said.

A Chouette Publishing adaptation of the original text by Francine Allen, based on the CAILLOU animated film series produced by CINAR Corporation (© 1997 Caillou Productions Inc., a subsidiary of CINAR Corporation). All rights reserved.
Original scenario written by Matthew Cope.
Illustrations taken from the television series CAILLOU.
Graphic design: Monique Dupras
Computer graphics: Les Studios de la Souris Mécanique

Canadian Cataloguing in Publication Data

Allen, Francine, 1955-
Caillou and Rosie's doll
New rev. ed.
(Backpack Series)
Translation of: Caillou et la poupée
For children aged 3 and up.
Co-published by: CINAR Corporation.

ISBN 2-89450-354-7

1. Beauty culture – Juvenile literature. 2. Brothers and sisters – Juvenile literature. I. CINAR Corporation. II. Title. III. Series.

TT957.A4413 2002 j646.7'26 C2002-941167-X

Legal deposit: 2002

We gratefully acknowledge the financial support of BPIDP and SODEC for our publishing activities.

Printed in China
10 9 8 7 6 5 4 3 2 1